Peanut Butter and Toast is dedicated to:

Delilah, Daisy, Lilly, Tinker, Bella, Jackson, and Sabrina. Our dogs and cats. Yep that's a lot, but we love them all! Morgan also wants to make a special dedication to her mom: Mom, I love you past the moon and stars.

-Mike and Morgan

www.mascotbooks.com

Peanut Butter and Toast

For more information, please contact:
Mascot Books
560 Herndon Parkway #120
Herndon, VA 20170
info@mascotbooks.com

Library of Congress Control Number: 2017900631

CPSIA Code: PRT0417A
ISBN-13: 978-1-68401-179-7

Printed in the United States

Peanut Butter
and
TOAST

by Mike Alden & Morgan Sciucco

Illustrated by
Jaime Buckley

My name is Morgan.

...and I have a <u>terrific</u> dad.

He works very hard every day.
Best of all, he is always there for me.

He goes to all of my soccer games, he's even one of the coaches.

He takes me to the park
and the movies,

helps me with my homework,

and we always have fun.

But even though my dad is terrific, he isn't perfect. Sometimes he makes mistakes, sometimes he makes a mess in the house,

but he especially makes a messy mistake with MY peanut butter and toast.

My dad, you see, likes peanut butter, a little more than most. He would put peanut butter on practically ANYthing he eats...

He would put it on his steak,

and he especially loves it on cake!

He loves peanut butter crackers and even puts peanut butter on apples.

Many mornings when I wake up after a restful night's sleep, my dad prepares me breakfast.

Sometimes it is watermelon with strawberries, sometimes it is cereal with berries.

But what I like most is peanut butter and toast. Any kind of toast: white, wheat, multigrain, and even English muffins.

Sometimes in the morning when my tummy is grumbling, and I am hungry for something from the toaster,

I ask my dad to make me what I like the most—some peanut butter and toast.

But even when I ask for just a little, he always puts too much peanut butter on my toast.

I DO like peanut butter,
but not as much as my dad.

Silly dad, he loves his peanut butter and I love my toast.

But I love my DAD the most!

About the Authors

Michael Alden is one of America's most popular direct-response hosts and personalities and founder and CEO of Blue Vase Marketing, a multimillion-dollar direct response company. He's also the bestselling author of *Ask More, Get More* and *5% More*. When he's not building one of the fastest growing companies in America, he's a wonderful father to an even more wonderful daughter.

You can find Mike on:
Instagram @MikeAlden2012
SnapChat @MikeAlden2012
Twitter @MikeAlden2012
Musical.ly @Mikealden2012
Facebook /MikeAlden2012

Morgan Sciucco is not only a children's book author, she is a student, athlete, and a drummer. Morgan has learned from her mom and dad that the sky is not the limit...it's only the beginning. She also has learned from both her mom and dad that hard work and dedication is important in anything you do.

You can find Morgan on:
Instagram @MorganNSciucco
Musical.ly @MorganSciucco

About the Illustrator

Jaime Buckley is an illustrator, author, and father of twelve. Originally a comic book artist, he's best known for his world of Wanted Hero and the comical fantasy series *Chronicles of a Hero*. In 2004, his fiction website, WantedHero.com attracted more than 750,000 visitors within the first twelve months. A proud grandfather of seven grandchildren, he lives in Utah with his wife Kathilynn and their nine children still at home.

Have a book idea?
Contact us at:

info@mascotbooks.com | www.mascotbooks.com